In memory of my father
and with gratitude for Terry, Eric, Nancy, Elena, and Kirsten. —B.F.

For the five little crows in our life, Napoleon, Ronin, Juliette, Valentine, and Lumiere.
With special thanks to Beth, Nancy, and Chelsea. —E.F. and T.F.

The Scarecrow
Text copyright © 2019 by Beth Ferry
Illustrations copyright © 2019 by Eric Fan and Terry Fan
All rights reserved. Manufactured in China.
No part of this book may be used or reproduced in any manner whatsoever without
written permission except in the case of brief quotations embodied in critical articles
and reviews. For information address HarperCollins Children's Books, a division of
HarperCollins Publishers, 195 Broadway, New York, NY 10007.
www.harpercollinschildrens.com

Library of Congress Control Number: 2018958690
ISBN 978-0-06-247576-3

The artists used pencil, ballpoint, and Photoshop to create the illustrations for this book.
Design by Chelsea C. Donaldson
19 20 21 22 23 SCP 10 9 8 7 6 5 4 3 2 1
❖
First Edition

THE SCARECROW

written by BETH FERRY   illustrated by THE FAN BROTHERS

HARPER

An Imprint of HarperCollinsPublishers

Autumn sunshine.
Haystacks rolled.
Scarecrow guards the fields of gold.

No one enters.

No one dares.

Scarecrow stands alone and scares

the fox and deer,

the mice and crows.

It's all he does. It's all he knows.

He never rests.

He never bends.

He's never had a single friend,

for all the woodland creatures know

not to mess with old Scarecrow.

Winter whispers.
    Velvet snow.
Scarecrow has no place to go.
He dreams of what the spring will bring
    of buds and blooms and things that sing.

Then something drops from midair.

A small, scared crow lying there.
Broken nest?
Broken wing?

Scarecrow does the strangest thing.
He snaps his pole,
   bends down low,
      saves the tiny baby crow.

He tucks him near his heart of hay.

He lets him sleep.

He lets him stay.

He doesn't stop to wonder why.

He sings the sweetest lullaby.

Safe and warm, the nestling mends.

These two make the oddest friends,

    but friends they are, right from the start.

The crow will grow in Scarecrow's heart.

And he will peek out at the farm,
  and he will perch on Scarecrow's arm.
And they will laugh and wish on stars,
  forgetting who they really are,

for crows are birds and birds must fly.
The fledgling spreads his wings to try.

He dips, then soars, and caws out loud.
Scarecrow cheers, pleased and proud,
but as he watches, Scarecrow knows
that he must stay and Crow must go.

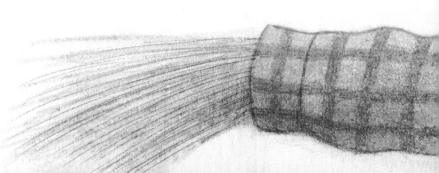

Summer sunshine.

Autumn chill.

Snowflakes make it colder still.

No one visits.

No one cares.

Scarecrow sags alone and stares.

Broken heart.
Broken pole.

Nothing fills the empty hole.

Then something drops from midair.
A large black crow standing there.

Scarecrow's arms are open wide.

Crow spreads his wings and swoops inside.

Joyful hearts.

Brimming hole.

A friend will mend a broken pole.

And he will spruce up matted hay,

and he will say,

"I'm here to stay."

Winter's over.

Springtime's due.

Is there room enough for two?

Flowers blooming.
Fields of green.
Five small eggs are tucked,
unseen.

Scarecrow guards them,
for he knows
that soon they will be
baby crows.

And he will love them from the start,
and they will grow up in his heart.

And they will peep and perch and play
and make him happy every day.
And as the seasons come and go,
they will love their dear Scarecrow.